This Books Belongs To:

ELLFOT BROWN
EISENBERG

Based on the original book of Peter Pan written
by J. M. Barrie

Special thanks to Nancy Hansen and Joyce Laveman
for their editorial assistance and general support for
this book project

For information regarding permission write:
Books to Bed, Inc.
224 West 35th Street, Room 700, New York, NY.10001

Library of Congress Cataloging-in-Publication Data on file
ISBN 978-1-61539-633-7

First Edition

Importer: Books to Bed, Inc.
Printed in China (Shenzhen)
BATCH NO. BA0906001TP
Recommended for age 3+

Visit www.Bookstobed.com

PETER PAN

Retold in Rhyme by:
Ilene Bauer

Jill Cozza-Turner

Illustrated By:
Alisa Grodsky

The Darling children –
  Wendy, Michael, and John
  were asleep with their pajamas on.
Their parents said good night to them
  without a sound,
Knowing they'd be safe
  when their dog Nana was around.

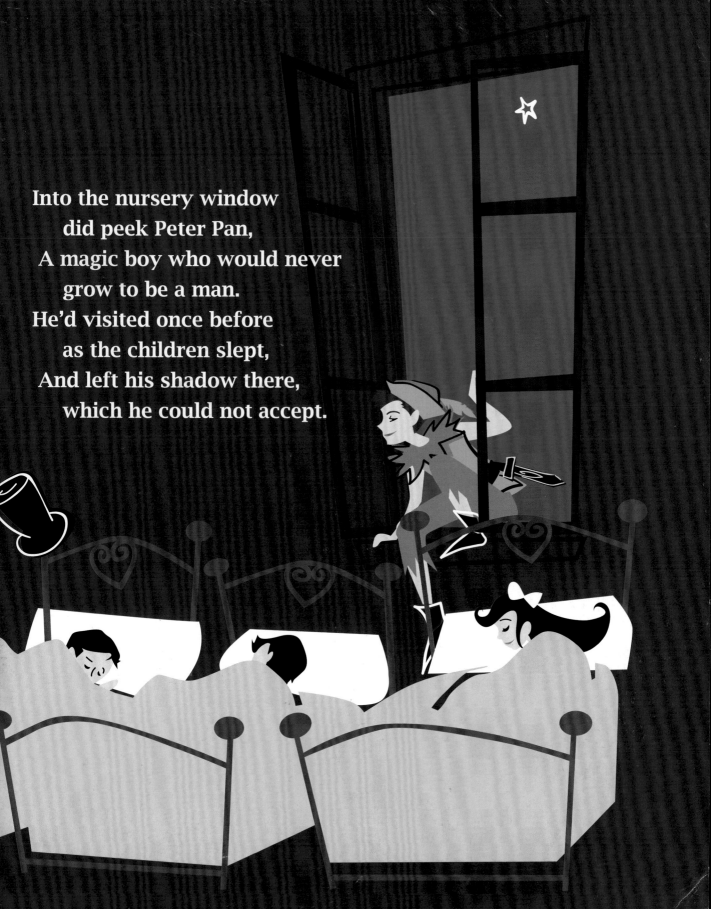

Into the nursery window
   did peek Peter Pan,
A magic boy who would never
   grow to be a man.
He'd visited once before
   as the children slept,
And left his shadow there,
   which he could not accept.

Wendy woke up with a start
and gasped in great surprise.
Her brothers jumped up too,
because they heard
her frightened cries.
Peter told them not to worry –
he would soon be gone
if only Wendy would agree
to sew his shadow on.

The children had such fun
    they begged him not to leave,
So Peter used some fairy dust
    he'd found hidden up his sleeve.
He sprinkled it upon them
    so that they all could fly,
And with Tinkerbell, his fairy friend,
    they soared into the sky.

Peter took them to his home,
   a magic place called Neverland.
The Darling children loved it there -
   they thought that it was grand!
They met Peter's friends, the Lost Boys,
   who were living underground,
And watched the children as they chased
   each other all around.

The Lost Boys looked to Wendy
    as the mom they never knew;
She read to them and taught them things,
    They loved her through and through.
In thanks they built
    a house for her
    so she would always stay,
And every day was special,
    just like a holiday.

In Neverland there were adventures
all the time,
With mermaids, and so many
rocks and trees to climb.
But no place can be perfect,
Peter had one bitter foe,
The awful Captain Hook,
whom he battled long ago.

In that angry struggle,
   Hook lost his precious hand.
It was swallowed by a crocodile
   who thought it tasted grand!
The croc also ate a clock
   on that fateful day,
Whenever Hook heard the ticking
   he knew to run away.
The pirate wanted sweet revenge,
   so he hatched an evil plan,
To kidnap dear sweet Wendy
   and hurt poor Peter Pan.

TICK TOCK

CLAP! CLAP! CLAP!

Hook's pirates also had a plan,
  they plotted on their ship.
They put poison in the glass of water
  that Peter was to sip.
Tinkerbell found out
  and to save her dearest friend,
She drank the water which was
  to be Peter's bitter end.

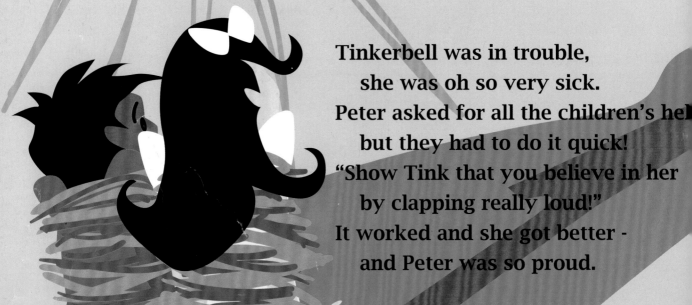

Tinkerbell was in trouble,
  she was oh so very sick.
Peter asked for all the children's hel
  but they had to do it quick!
"Show Tink that you believe in her
  by clapping really loud!"
It worked and she got better -
  and Peter was so proud.

But Pan's work was not over,
  Wendy needed his help too.
Peter pushed Hook off the plank
  and came to to her rescue.
As Hook fell to the water
  he heard that old "tick-tock."
It was his dreaded enemy -
  the pirate-eating croc!

The adventure was now over,
it was time to go back home.
Wendy asked Peter Pan to come,
but from Tink he could not roam.
Pan stayed in Neverland,
and he bid his friends goodbye.
But the Lost Boys were so sad
they couldn't help but cry.

The Darlings were
   so grateful
   their kids finally returned;
But when they listened to the tale,
   they were filled
   with deep concern.

So they took in all the Lost Boys,
and happy they've since been;
But sometimes at the window
there is Peter peeking in...